The House

Paul Carro

For information contact :
paulcarrohorror@gmail.com

Or visit: paulcarrohorror.com

ISBN: 978-1-7350701-0-0

PREFACE

I consume horror, horror endures. I began consuming horror at an early age via movie theaters, VHS, specialty shops, magazines like *Fangoria*, comic books, and amusement parks. But before all that I dipped my toe into scary waters through the written word. I learned at an early age to see Jane run and before too long it became see Jane run—from alien invaders stealing human bodies. The works of Poe, James, Bradbury, Koontz, King, Serling, Matheson, Shelley, and so many others infected me like a zombie plague from the first inked pages.

In my years of reading ghoulish tales, there has been much debate about what classifies as horror. To me, if it unsettles, forces me to question reality, makes me see shapes where there are none, or keeps me fearfully awake all night, I file it away as horror. While I like my movies bloody, books need not be so as they have other tools which can cut deeper than sharpened knives—well-chosen words. While in high school, I frequented a local bookstore (who identified me as the resident horror addict). They picked my brain like a zombie on a bender to determine which books they should order. Our collaboration resulted in a wonderfully curated horror section. I was proud of the deep cuts I brought to my local reading spot.

Then the crash. Over time horror fell from favor. Many bookstores eliminated the category, filing the frightful gems away in the oddest of sections. (I don't think books about serial killers should be in the self-help section, but what do I know?) I still sought my fix no matter where employees might have hidden the twisted tales (contingent on any being there at all). As time wore on, the genre went absent altogether in some bookstores. Sometimes horror goes away.

While there is a renaissance now, we must nurture it lest it fade away again. I am finally writing in my favorite genre. My intention is to announce it directly on the book-cover. The words, 'A Horror Novel,' will adorn my front covers so if ever people become too scared to celebrate horror again, if they try to bury the medium like a rotting corpse, it will be a little easier to find. This is my first horror novel, but trust me, there will be more. I hope by my chosen words I will unsettle you, frighten you, unnerve or unmoor you. The ultimate win would be if I created a 'freezer book' for even one reader. (A book which frightens someone so much they hide it in the freezer.)

All authors have access to the same twenty-six letters. The writers I listed above know how to arrange them just right. They are the masters and I am their student. This is the start of my journey into horror. Hang on, because if you ride this out with me, I expect it will be a hell of a ride.

I consume horror, horror endures.

To Mom who started this all and left far too soon.